For David, Megan and Mary

First published 1995 by
Walker Books Ltd, 87 Vauxhall Walk
London SE11 5HJ

This edition published 1996

2 4 6 8 10 9 7 5 3

© 1995 John Prater

This book has been typeset in Century Old Style.

Printed in Hong Kong

British Library Cataloguing in Publication Data
A catalogue record for this book is
available from the British Library.

ISBN 0-7445-4359-2

Ringling Bros. and Barnum & Bailey

THE GREATEST SHOW ON EARTH

JOHN PRATER

WALKER BOOKS
AND SUBSIDIARIES
LONDON • BOSTON • SYDNEY

Ladies and gentlemen, boys and girls, welcome to the circus!
It's the greatest show on earth.
There's magic and daring, amazing acts and incredible tricks …

and there's Harry. That's me!

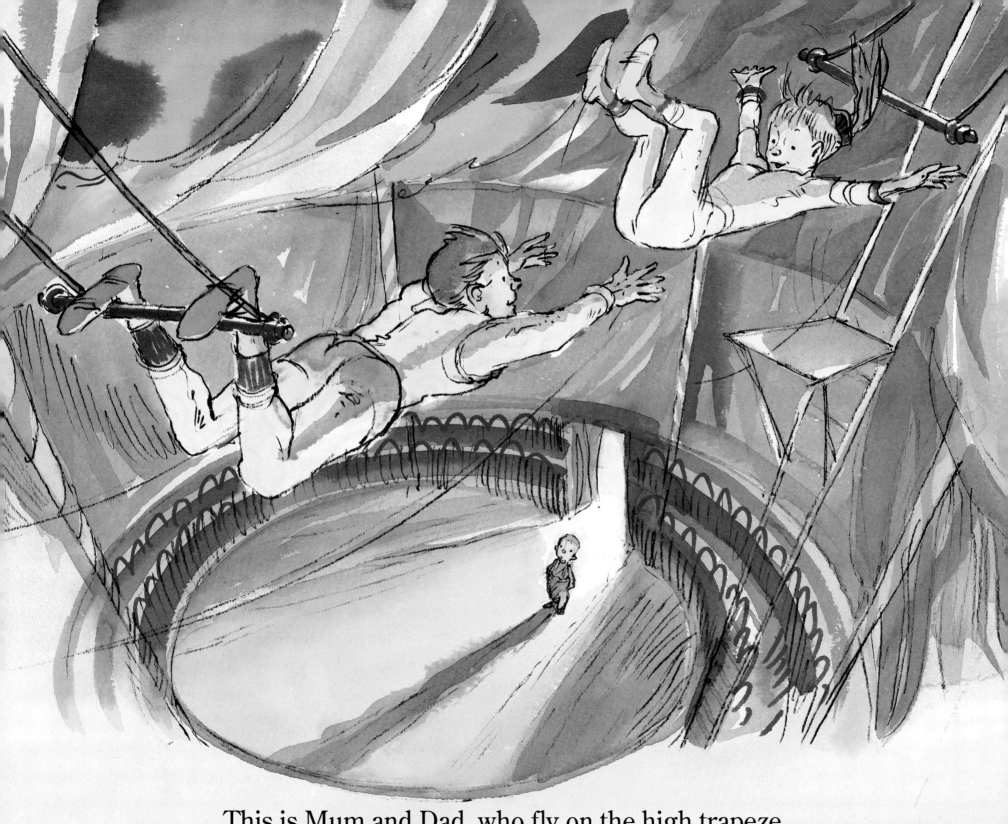

This is Mum and Dad, who fly on the high trapeze.

And this is me… Oops!

This is my brilliant sister Sue. She can juggle almost anything.

And this is me… Ouch!

This is Wobble and Wilt – the cleverest acrobats you've ever seen.

And this is me… Whoops!

Abracadabra! This is Mr Mysterio conjuring flowers and fireworks from his hat.

And this is me… Bang!

This is Grandad on his wild whizzing wheels.

And this is me… Oooer! Yikes!

This is Grandma, who's so strong she can lift a trailer with one hand.

And this is me... Oh, dear!

And this is Wellington the dog. He tops the bill with his amazing balancing act. I can't fly through the air or juggle or balance or do magic tricks, so I look after Wellington.

This is me.

Tonight's the night of the big show.
Ladies and gentlemen, boys and girls, silence, please,
for Wellington's amazing balancing act!

But Wellington sees a mouse and… WOOF! SQUEAK! "Oh, no!"

CLATTER! WHOOSH! "Help!"

BOING! WHEE! "I'm flying!"

SWOOSH! SWING! "This is fun!"

WOBBLE! WHIZZ! "I can do it! Hooray!"

Hooray for Mum and Dad, the fliers; my sister Sue, the juggler; Wobble and Wilt, the acrobats; Mr Mysterio, the magician; Grandad, the trick cyclist; Grandma, the strongwoman; my dog Wellington who walks the wire … and who else?

Let's hear it now! As loud as you can!
HOORAY FOR HARRY THE CLOWN!
That's me!

MORE WALKER PAPERBACKS
For You to Enjoy

ONCE UPON A TIME
by Vivian French/John Prater

A little boy tells of his "dull" day, while all around a host
of favourite nursery characters act out their stories.

"The pictures are excellent, the telegraphic text perfect, the idea brilliant. We have here a classic,
I'm sure, with an author-reader bond as strong as *Rosie's Walk*." *Books for Keeps*

0-7445-3690-1   £4.50

GRANDAD'S MAGIC
by Bob Graham

Grandad's magic may not be big magic, but it's large enough
to cause a stir in Alison's house one Sunday lunchtime!

"Full of neat asides and significant details... Excellent." *The Times Educational Supplement*

0-7445-1471-1   £3.99

MONKEY TRICKS
by Camilla Ashforth

Shortlisted for the Children's Illustrated Book of the Year (British Book Awards)

Horatio, the rabbit, and James, the bear, are the best of friends. Their peaceful world is turned
upside-down, though, when mischievous monkey Johnny Conqueror appears, full of tricks!

"A remarkable new talent... Picture-book publishing at its best." *The Economist*

0-7445-3168-3   £4.50

Walker Paperbacks are available from most booksellers, or by post from B.B.C.S., P.O. Box 941, Hull, North Humberside HU1 3YQ

24 hour telephone credit card line 01482 224626

To order, send: Title, author, ISBN number and price for each book ordered, your full name and address, cheque or postal order payable to BBCS for the total amount and allow the following for postage and packing:
UK and BFPO: £1.00 for the first book, and 50p for each additional book to a maximum of £3.50.
Overseas and Eire: £2.00 for the first book, £1.00 for the second and 50p for each additional book.

Prices and availability are subject to change without notice.